DESTINY

THE SET RIGHT FORCE

JUNO ASHOK

Made with ♥ on the Notion Press Platform
www.notionpress.com

To the forever support of mine...

Amma and Appa

Friends who believed in me!

Contents

FOREWORD

"Destiny- The set right force -gave the spark ... Admired by the way, You described the quests of universe in the story of **Sarah**. you got the voice of universe ,didn't you ?Another insightfull book from you. Loved reading every single lines .starting from the realistic scenarios happening at all homes to ending with mysterious destiny,you led amazingly with the story lines ,that flowed with the unexpected twists and turns.That curiosity travelled with me till the end. The Theme you used to describe destiny is amazing. Undoubtedly Every line of your book shows your compassion about the theme..which I love too.. As usual your lines directly hits the soul of Readers...happy writing.. loved your work...Believe in Universe."- ***B.J.Harini, Graphophile***

"Great work Juno. Yet another masterpiece from the author of diary of predilected didactics that stole my heart. It took me away to Sarah's world. The starting part was quite relatable and focus on the finer details gave the feel of oneness with the story. And then came the unexpected twist. Awestruck with ur words as usual. I literally travel through your stories every time. And this one didn't even allow me to move making my hands numb!"

- ***Varshinee G***

A Readaholic

PREFACE

Some beautiful beginnings are often underestimated. Some dreadful beginning have been over rated. Yet we all run in a race where we often don't even know where we are heading to.

But somehow one way or the other we all end up reaching a place which may be the one we wished for or may not be. Yet when looked into deeply we will find that it is either the one which is far better or the worse to make us the best after all.

what is your desperation? do you have one towards which you are running with a passion? If so, do you think your destiny is also the same?

Let's explore what is destined for this temporary Earth stay of ours'!

ACKNOWLEDGEMENTS

Those little troop of mine who went busy helping me in the mess of designing this book and sat along with me listening my maniac all till dawn from dusk on the day of scribbling this!

-Anu ragavi akka, Jayavardhini and others!

Prologue

How far does your imagination go when you are wide awake yet not ready to get out of the bed during misty mornings? How far will you go to wish for the best dreams possible in your day dreaming classes and boring lecturess? What will be your dimesions and perspectives of sequences dashing through your mind while listening to music? How hard to try to match the visions of the fast forwarding outside eembellishments while travelling?

what if all of a sudden these become true? How would you react if all these became a nightmare alive? What will be your reaction if all these transform to be a sweet reality?

A whole lot of questions and cxpectations are encircling our life, dredging us out of various events and incidents. Do you trust your destiny which is dragging you in the troughs and crates of life?

Come let's give walk through the destiny of Sarah to know more and better!

I

The boarding

The divine music spreading all over with the sunlight breaking through the window and lighting the entire room; there she lay with her mind churning thoughts of every undiscovered field and her eyes scanning all the "never gonna attempt" stunts of cooking, crafts and other stuffs.

"Can't you just stop looking at that stupid piece of gadget and come help me in this!"

"Coming mom..." sighed Sarah and went to the kitchen

"Your dad needs to get ready in half an hour and I haven't completed the cooking. And you came back from college yet of no use. Sitting idle clutching the piece of modern devil and not even caring about your mother and her struggles. Why can't you just come and ask me whether I need any help?"

"MOM!! Please don't start in the morning... just tell me what I need to do" shouted Sarah irritably.

"These kids and their tongue!" sighed her mom and gave her some veggies to chop.

Sarah is the only daughter of Mr. and Mrs. Steven. After her resignation from the job she worked in, she has come for a short break before her next phase. Her mom and dad gave her all the freedom with limits and she was obviously enjoying the freedom and cursing the limits as all the common children do. She was pretty good at things yet was too docile to take them up.

She is a girl with passion who loves to explore things and make her master them. She quits when she feels her interest is being drained out, no matter what the consequnces may await her. Mrs. Steven is often worried about her behaviour of this. Being a typical Indian mother she want her daughter to adjust according to the situations and circumstances as she believes in the stereotyping ceremony of "girl tagging"

Mr. Steven is someone who is fond of his sweet daughter acting as a counter push to Mrs.Steven, encouraging Sarah in all possible ways. He feels proud whenever Sarah achieves something high alongside the tag "SARAH STEVEN". He never questions Sarah and her decisions and often stands with her no matter what. Sarah instead always makes sure that she never makes her parents and especially dad feel low about her and her decisions.

The previous job she worked in gave her ample amount of experience both in life and work, which made her confident enough to come up with the decision of resignation considering the fact that she deserve something better and upgraded.

“We will be going to our native tonight... make sure you guys keep everything ready” said her dad in a stern tone, an odd event of stern voice especially when Sarah is out there.

“But dad... I came back just two days ago... a long travel again... no please!” cried Sarah. Actually that wasn’t the sole and true reason for her denial. Native place equals no privacy for her to enjoy, with relatives and kids buzzing and bullying. She is the oldest among all the cousins and hence more responsibilities and sincerity over her crown to bear.

Eventhough her mind hated it, the only thing it loves about her native is the ambience over there. The greenery all around to accompany her during the hot scar rupturing words of all the old ones there. She loves wandering all around engaging her soul with fresh air to breathe and calmness to adore. Interupting her lane of analysis came the soft and crisp voice of her dad.

“We will definitely be back within your break this time... Okay?” pacified her dad. Of course being a girl child, she was showered with all his love and she was a princess to her dad.

Her mom wasn’t convinced. She stared Steven for a moment and started the spark for the day’s fire.

"so you want me and my daughter to come and toil again among those piercing words, right? you and your relatives making fun of everything, mocking at how I pampered Sarah eventhough everybody know that I did the right thing!"

Sarah gave a look of ashtoinishment when her mom gave a sudden side shift fom scolding her to joing her as "me and my daughter"

"It’s not what I wish to... but we are supposed to go and that’s it!" Steven raised a note higher.

"Don’t you remember!! your mom and her..."

Sarah sensed the rising tension and dived in to change the mood.

"Oh no! dad! I need many things to be added as I thought I'm gonna be in home, I didn’t bring anything back from my stay place."

"Chalo na mom! come let’s have a look. Mom your milk in the stove is burning I guess! Isn’t is right dad?"

"YEAH!!"

"Yes ... it burns like my stomach and no one understands that!" grumbled Mrs.Steven and turned around.

Sarah put in her list of things and took her mom in winking to her dad.

“Hoof.... What a busy bee day with crumbling hurdles of emotional dramas!” said her mind. She wasn’t a girl who is interested in dramatic emotions especially in her home but her heart was deeply connected with one soul. The love of her life where all her melo dramas will be admired by the other!

II

Unpacking and Repacking

Some vibes can be unmatched and one among them is the divine vibe. The sounds of hymns and forever calm gripped enclosure is something which every mind deserves to be at times.

Sarah was in the mid of life's glass bridge with the cracks in it hindering her to move forward. Eventhough she was determined to finish this off today, something made her make the series of pause and resume battles.

With a divine music and blended emotions onlooking the crusified christ above, Sarah wasn't expecting the first twist of destiny on that day. The grace of God being explained behind and many pairs of hands and eyes devoted to it, something made her heart throb and jump abnormally. Her mind was chocked with thoughts and confusions on the decision status updated to be "pending".

"Listen... it's not about your surroundings it's about you and what you decide... I want YOUR answer and not others'" said Adam in a firm voice.

Adam was her church friend whom she had shared a lot and who is now in turn asking her to share her life with him. He was indeed a good looking guy with the best characters yet she wasn't sure whether she could decide and recite a positive or negative nod. She liked him yet was indulged in the fear of the usual family ethics and protocols. She had said the same to him too for which came the above reply.

"I need time and I need courage. I lack both now. What am I supposed to do?"

"See I can understand your situation, yet it is in YOUR hands and you are supposed to decide what the hell is good for you Sarah!" shouted Adam losing his patience after explaining her for about a year and a half.

Deep in her mind she was startled, confused, angry, sad and every kind of emotional roller coaster thriving one after other. Adam was the one in whom she hadn't seen a different version according to changing situations.

But now for the first time when it came to be his decision, he started showing up himself as a commoner in her view. The special place of 'ONE WHO UNDERSTANDS ALL OF MY SITUATIONS" transformed to become "THE COMMONER AGAIN". she couldn't utter a word against him and so she sat there staring at the tiled floor as if she saw it for the first time.

Kindled by her silence he stood up and shouted in his highest voice

"YOU ARE GONNA REGRET THIS! I'M SURE YOU WILL. YOU ARE LOSING SUCH A GOOD LIFE. YOU... WILL... REGRET..!!!"

As if petrified Sarah was looking in shock at Adam. She hadn't seen Adam in such a mood or saying such harsh words to her in the entire journey with him.

"Yes! I did make him lose his patience but I was refusing to accept because I know I can't. He was the one forcing me to rethink twice thrice and n times again and I did it for heaven's sake. Then why and what is my mistake?!"

With her mind battling for words and eyes welling up to blur her vision, her mouth mumbled the words

"YES I REGRET! Not for losing you but for having such a manipulator beside me all these times"

So destiny had other plans for her hope so? of course it had!

III

The resume

The thoughts of her and her not so bitter yet twisted past were disturbed by her mom asking her to choose the colour of dress she want to pack for her. Of course, native place with a big chunk of houses to visit and relatives to greet and meet, the requirements also seemed to be so big and uneneding. Her mom made sure that they chose bright coloured traditional attires as she doesn't wanna spare a single reason for her co -sisters and sisterly sisters of the sisters and sisters blame her.

It is quite common to hear those words of sharpness yet she chose not to poke into that this time. Sarah knew very well that this determination of "not to poke" won't last long but still she doesn't want get herself into trouble by counteracting her mom.

"This is for nanny's house... this one for uncle's... this one for nithu's... this one for sharmi's.. this one is for roshan's and this one a spare if we need.. all done I guess... Sarahh!! Aren't you done yet?"

"Yes mom... almost..." hurried Sarah brushing aside her thoughts and stuffing her cloths in her bag.

"Make sure you choose bright colours. Don't come and stand in front as if we don't provide you cloths and getting yours' from the thrift!"

"Okay mom... please don't say that for a million times!" came an irritated response from Sarah.

"Even after a millionth time... you still choose to be like a beggar on street with torn clothes!"

Sensing the tensed air, she chose to shut up and not to start an argument again. As she was about to push all those clothes in, there came a smile in her face seeing her black saree which she kept in. Though she know that the feel is something wierd, she loved it much and hence she clutched it hard not to let it go at any cost.

And thus goes the reason behind her smile...

"Please don't say me you took up my side!"

"Of course I did, why won't I?"

"Are you mad or something?"

"Yes I am!"

"Excuse me?"

"I'm mad about you Sarah. Yes I know the entire project team would make me go down in the next meeting for supporting you. But I truly don't care. All I need is you and your support which can make me overcome anything."

His determined voice made her entire system stand still for a second. Her heart raced fast for a battle with her brain which was busy arguing that this is again a trap like the previous one. Her heart wasn't ready to completely refuse the stand yet was also not ready to accept it either.

She was busy churning questions like " what if he is like Adam?" "what if I say the same statement as I did with Adam?" "will I ever able to face him again?" "what if this was a trap for something else?" "will he even care about my parent's opinion?" "what if this was some kind of a prank?"

She who was already tired of thinking a solution to the mess she made in her office which was in the verge of pushing her to get fired. She lost her project pendrive and was both showered with the angry vibes of her boss and team mates. And now here stood Kevin taking her side and saving her and her job. This will never be welcomed by her team mates as she being a busy bee strict lead, she wasn't so friendly with all.

"Done?"

"What?"

"Don't ever think I will accept on hearing your story. You supported me and my forever gratitude for that. But never think I will say yes for this!"

"I don't want you to say yes for me taking your side. I will take your side even if you say no and even if you hate me so"

"But why?" came a confused odd look from Sarah as this seemed to be the pole opposite to her previous experience and perspective.

"I want you to be happy and I want that happiness to be mine. That is all I wish for. And nothing more is what I expect!"

"What if I say a no... what if I say I fear my family" questioned Sarah with a mind to reveal his true face. But wasn't prepared to expect the twist awaiting.

"I will still remain the same but with a boundary called "distance""

"So you don't care about my family's acceptance, don't you?"

"Yes I do... and I surely can manage that... but for all I need your support too"

"you do care about their opinion?" she couldn't believe her ears.

"Of course I do and I should"

"Why?"

"It is them who gave you life and it is them who gave you all of their love and trust. And it is mandatory to respect them and their decisions which is the foremost one!"

"What if they say no?"

"That is when they aren't satisfied. Why should we make them feel bad about us? We can together make them feel good about us?" came a calm and cool response from him.

Sarah couldn't think of something better than these words. She felt something hard saying her to trust the process holding Kevin's hand till the end and thus started the beautiful love steps without courage picking up its pace along the course. And hope the reason for her smile is now justified!

May is this what destiny planned for her and her love?!

IV

The turn 1

The beautiful morning of fresh air and transfixing scenario was interrupted by the ring of her customized song for Kevin. She was busy dreaming hard as she went to a state of unconsiousness out of the tired journey she had all way long. With voices interupting and disrupting her sleep more often, she was strong enough to overcome those disturbances and sleep to her might. But this ringtone of hers‘ is something which has the power to wake her up at any cost.

"Good morning your highness!" came a jumble bumble tone of Kevin.

"Oh shut up! Don't start your teasing ceremony right in the morning" said the sleepy squeak of Sarah.

"Highness... it is the high time to join in your meeting link with a high degree of responsibility if you have a high level of anxiety about your team and their high ended project ahead"

"what... high... me... time... meeting... shit!!" jumped Sarah from her bed not realizing she is on her break and needn't worry about meetings and targets.

Kevin had a good laugh sensing her sudden leap of tension and calmed her down.

"Chill down Sarah... YOU ARE ON YOUR BREAK IDIOT!"

"KEVIN... STOP MAKING FUN OF ME!"

"Okayy okayyy sorry miss... go and have a good day sleep... bye"

"bye"

She couldn't lay down further after being waken up like this wide enough, she went out of the room to witness a troop of people blended with all age groups sitting over there. The oldest ones with serious looks, the middle aged ones with laughter and sarcastic talks; the youngest ones with fun topics and the teeny meeny ones with their play time atrocities. She could sense the usual and casual happening in her native. She was used to this and forced a formality smile not knowing what else to do.

She was once among the group of teeny meeny ones not caring about anything and then in the youngest phase enjoying after answering the interview session about the academics; now in between the youngest and the middle, the most dangerous phase of all.

"And what's next Sarah?" chuckled the unknown uncle. To Sarah all the men side is uncles and the women side is aunties without any discrimination as she knows none of them for god's sake.

"Work uncle" said Sarah in an irritated tone. She knew that everyone there know that yet those teasy interrogations she face as a 'girl' everytime made her climb up in the ladder of anger.

"Say with respect Sarah" whispered her mom in her ears.

"Haan...haaan" sighed Sarah.

"My friend's son is placed in a better position than hers' with the same degree. Why can't you go further and try something better dear?"

"Oh my goodness. Here we go with the war of words with the swords of sarcasm degrading each others' kids in every possible instant" mumbled Sarah.

"Yeah uncle trying" cut Sarah with her responses as small as possible.

"Aren't your mom and dad feeding you beta? Why are you like this? You must put on some weight so that the groom searching would be easy for us" laughed an aunty who was struggling herself to fit in to the chair she occupied.

Before Sarah could storm in came Steven's response

"SARAH... GO INSIDE AND DO YOUR WORK... YOU HAVE WORK FROM HOME RIGHT?"

"Ye... yes dad... he.. here... bye.. yeah I'm going" went Sarah with a smile for her dad's timely protection.

"This IS why I hate coming here...!"

Saying so sarah saw her phone which gave her a notification saying "Missed call from K" 5 times.

"What the heck happened to him again?"

Dialing K...

"Sarahh... you... you won't believe me!!"

"What?! Why are you so serious?"

"Serious? Not serious actually... pretty excited to be precise"

"Whassup man?"

"I saw someone"

"And..?"

"She... she... shee.."

"So you are excited on seeing a girl other than me?" frowned Sarah

"She is you!"

"ARE YOU OKAY KEVI?"

"Yes I am... hey I ain't kidding... I saw you!"

"Something got into your mind stupid!"

"No... I saw a girl exactly like you.. the copy version of yours'... may be your twin!"

"WHAT ARE YOU BLABBERING?"

"I swear... I would have hugged her if I hadn't noticed her with the badge holding some other name!" said Kevin half serious and half playful in provoking her. He love playing with her and making her angry. To be precise he was fond of it.

"Mind you kevi!!" almost screaming Sarah burning with anger and possesiveness storming simulatneously.

"But its true... you don't trust me?"

"Nope!"

"Wait... I will send you a pic of her... "

Saying this Kevin cut the call abruptly not waiting for Sarah's reply.

"Another good day... another prank... this kevi is just..." smiling to herself she saw the message. Opening it was the biggest mistake she did. The turn of her life. She saw a mirror image of her somehow managed, a long shot, in different clothes with a badge named "SERENE"

V

The halt

Sarah's hands were trembling as she saw her duplicate. She couldn't even think of a response for that when Kevin called her tired of waiting for the response. How could one react if they see themselves staring at themselves but in a different way that they know that they aren't themself.

"Hey... did you see her... same na?" excited Kevin was texting her hurriedly one after the other.

"Kevi... please say this is a prank!" she almost cried

"NOOO... SARAH this is real!" jumped Kevin.

"Where the hell are you now?"

"She is the owner of the farms near which I have bought a hill house! I saw her today as I came here to enjoy the break with my parents. At first I thought you lied about your native and you are here to surprise me... and then as I neared here I sensed it was the other case. She IS YOUR REPLICA!"

"Many say, seeing your replica is kinda exciting but you know what...it isn't... it is horror striking to see someone in your body... I mean... you can understand what I mean... I guess..."

"Yes yes... calm down Sarah... I will interact with her and make you speak with her... it will be nice if you get to know each other... and also..."

"Also?"

"I may get a better option in choosing between you and your replica!!" giggled Kevin.

"You will be pacified Mr.Kevin"

"Sure I know your highness... just a joke... will call u back!"

"Okay!!"

Though the phone hanged, she couldn't get through that. She was truly panic stricken. She was dreadfully waiting for Kevin to call back.

Back in hills...

The breeze and the green leaves rattle was so pleasant that nobody could deny the beauty. The hill house stood in the top with a breath taking view making one's mind go to a state of naturistic enlightment. Kevin was focusing hard to get a better view of his love's replica and was so excited in enjoying the moment too.

Serene on the other hand was busy making arrangements for their new farm. She seemed to be a strong girl and the determined look in her face made her even more powerful. She was steady and her formal attire and neatly brushed hair made her look like a doll given a life. Though she was the replica of Sarah, she had something in her which can made anyone go and approach her atleast for a decent talk without any seconds' consideration. Kevin though was hesitant at first to start a conversation, somehow managed to near her and open his mouth.

"Hey miss... I am Kevin from the next door... may I have a word with you?"

"yeah Mr.Kevin... nice meeting you... but I am so sorry... I have no time having words with strangers like you" came an attitude heaped reply for the other end.

Though irritated, Kevin kept his voice low. His high regard for her took a leap down and he gave a stern look in return.

"I can understand but it is regarding Sarah... I mean your replica... sorry look a like or whatever!"

"Excuse me?" came a question with even more strong questioning eyes.

"Yes... I know someone who looks exactly the same like you!"

"I DON'T HAVE TIME FOR THIS STUPIDITY!" shouted Serene all of a sudden.

"Either do I miss!! It is true and Sarah is my girlfriend!" equally raising Kevin as he had never felt so offended in front of a girl like this.

"What do you want now?" asked Serene with a tone of carelessness which even more triggered Kevin. He would have walked away leaving her behind but stood there thinking of the tensed face of Sarah which would be there awaiting him and his response.

"Just look at this!" saying so Kevin showed a pic of Sarah beaming beautifully. A wave of shock spread over the face of the onlooker.

"WHAT DID YOU SAY HER NAME IS?"

"Sarah! Why" agitated by her attitude, he was not in the mood to answer her.

"I need to meet her immediately... no matter what!" came a serious and sincere response which was totally ironical.

Kevin was startled. He did expect a reaction but not this much.

"You can talk to her now if you wish... but..."

"Don't you hear me...? I WANNA MEET HER RIGHT NOW!"

This seemed to be the face two of her something terrific and shaking.

Sensing something serious Kevin called Sarah

"Yes kevi... can I speak to her?"

"SERENE WANTS TO MEET YOU SARAH!"

VI

The kick start

“Why should I meet her?” “what is the need to meet her?” and “why is she so tensed?” “why did she captivate Kevin when I said I am not ready to meet her?” with strangling questions and revolving answers she boarded the bus to SERENE FARMS of Nilgiris.

Sarah was in the height of confusion. She couldn’t believe her ears when she heard the statement "If you need your Kevin just come here immediately!"

Sarah who was not so good in giving reasons for trip and that too being in her native which is an added and biggest hurdle of all. She somehow managed to make her parents believe that she ought to go immediately and started her journey to the fascinating hill station which had its own twists and turns but not more than those awaiting her on the top of it.

the beautiful scenery was her least concern which used to be her foremost even when Kevin is around. She was horrified, confused, soaked in tears and nothing was able to explain her feeling more precisely. With all her wandering thoughts scavenging her she finally managed to go up to the entrance and start her impatient journey by her conversation.

After several questions to the security and after answering the return rapid fire from the higher authorities inside, she was allowed to meet Serene. With anger overcoming excitement, she stepped into her room.

"LEAVE KEVIN RIGHT NOW MISS.SER...."

Her eyes seemed to be petrified. She witnessed herself sitting in front of her with confidence a hundred fold and attitude a thousand fold increased. She couldn't believe her eyes for the second time yet reality of Kevin's captivation hit her and she was about to storm again when the bold voice of the other end welcomed her.

"Oh my goodness... you... literally are... yes... Kevin is right... he..." stammered Serene for the first time hope so.

"Cut the crap! Where is Kevin?" came a sharp and hard question.

"Sarah... please calm down..." came Serene as if she was trying to pacify her.

"Why the hell should I witch!"

"Okay... you may call me whatever you like as I am your sister!" came a calm reply with a grin from Serene.

"WHAT?!!" came an ashtonished reply from Sarah.

"Yes Sarah... you are my long lost sister. My very own sister" banged Serene with her arms cletching the stress ball as hard as she could.

Saying so came Serene to give her a hug. But furious Sarah wasn't ready to accept the hospitality.

"I NEED TO SEE KEVIN!"

Kevin- kevin- kevin is all her mind was filled with such that nothing could intrude her at any time.

"Of course you can... But..."

"What do you need... come straight to the point" twisted Sarah with the top notch tense tone.

"That's so nice of my sissy"

Serene seemed to provoke her to the core as if she was only interested in. Sarah was fuming with anger making her burst out.

"First of all I AM NOT YOUR SISSY!"

"Lemme explain that to you sweetheart. You and me are identical twins. We were on a trip to this same hills and our mom and dad lost me... I was taken by this farm owner and I was brought up by him as his own daughter... but I got to know the truth an year ago... yet out of gratitude I don't wanna upset my father by saying I wanna meet my biological parents and that is why I didn't attempt of finding you all... but destiny has other plans I guess... and it made me meet you out of no where"

"NO YOU... YOU ARE... YOU ARE LYING...!"

"This is the truth sarah" slammed Serene hard on the table.

"But I haven't seen you in any of my childhood photos. Your identity wasn't shown to me even a glimpse after these many years!" mumbled Sarah who was overwhelming with the spring of confusion.

"That is for your well being Sarah... a twin cannot live without the other right!"

"But if you were my twin... my mom and dad wouldn't have let you down so soon like that?"

"OUR mom and dad, Sarah!"

"Answer?!"

"may be... the answer is theirs'"

Sarah felt like something is pushing her from all directions. She fainted!

VII

The rough path

Sarah witnessed Serene hugging her parents. They were with happy tears and all the relatives she hated were so nice to her. Sarah felt she was left all alone all of a sudden. She saw Serene with a wicked smile looking at her. She started shouting "Just listen to me... please" "I'm here mom... dad!!" "please" "please"

"Sarah... are you okay?" came serene's voice with a fake accent of "twin care" trying to wake her up from shouting and bringing her back to reality.

Though Sarah couldn't differentiate the true and fake care, she lay there with a weak body. She couldn't look at her and she was not ready to protest either. All she could do was to cry and she did it too. She was now ready to surrender and started asking with a feeble voice.

"What do you want? Please leave Kevin!" cried sarah with tears wetting up her cushion.

"Sarah... please don't cry... I didn't mean to make my twin cry!" hugged Serene with a soothing voice and comforting tone. Yet she was not ready to trust her. Something made her stay away. And she trusted the vibes always which used to save her at many instances.

"Please leave Kevin"

"Sure... I will... I will... but on one condition... it is actually a request from my side!" demanded Serene. Sarah was actually expecting the threat yet she was also aware that she shouldn't give words as such and be careful.

"What do you want!!" came a little voice.

"I want you to stay here in my place for a week so that it doesn't upset my father and I want to witness the warmth of parental love too. I will take your place back there just for a week... I will not say the truth and I won't bother you ever again. Please let me stay with my parents for just a week..."

"NO WAY!! HOW COULD I STAY HERE AND LEAVE AN UNKNOWN TO TAKE MY PLACE!!"

"Sarah listen... I will not disturb your place their... neither you are gonna do here... just a week's stay and that too my father isn't here now... he will be back from his business trip after a week. I will be returning on the same day he does. All you need is to pretend that Serene is here. That's it!"

"ARE YOU MAD OR SOMETHING?!"

Sarah still couldn't believe her ears and was processing the request so hard in her brain.

"Any better suggestions?"

"Yes!! Better let us go together to my parents and say that your long lost child is back and will be with you for a week and go back to her guardian father!"

"What if our mom and dad doesn't allow me back? What if my father here knows about this and feel dejected? Is this what I have done in return to the man who showered me is love all these days and made me feel completely safe and rich?"

Sarah was confused. She couldn't risk either of the sides. She was about to cry and missed her mom and dad so much at the very moment. She thought that the very first drastic step she took without her parents permission ended up so badly.

"Will you Sarah?" interrogated Serene awaiting her answer.

"NOO" came a stern response from Serene. She wasn't ready to accept the fact of giving up her parents even for a week.

Then came a change in tone in Serene' the pacifying request turned into a hostage order.

"Right then. If you want your Kevin back ALIVE, do as I say! Got it damn?"

Sarah was petrified. She couldn't makeup where this is going and how this is taking her. She was in the verge of fainting again. She couldn't risk the life of Kevin either. She made up her mind and took a bold decision.

"FINE THEN! Juz a week and not even a second more. if you couldn't come back on time I will straight away board a bus and come back home revealing who you are?'

"SURE SARAHH... THANK YOU SO MUCH" came back her former self back to form. Sarah couldn't figure out what was happening. She was about to think that Serene was mentally disturbed.

"And... one more thing... I need Kevin to be with me all the time this entire week... I can't stay in this unknown place with complete set of strangers addressing with a stranger's name!" said Sarah with something up in her mind. But Serene out of sheer happiness couldn't and wasn't even ready to guess that.

"Yeah... sure... anything from my side!" said Serene with a happiest face. For a second or two Sarah herself on seeing the contented face thought that all these stuff are true and consoled her storming mind.

After a minute, came Kevin with a tired face accompanied by two guards. Sarah ran to him an gave him a hug with a sob. Kevin consoled her assuring his wellness when came in Serene with a lad.

"Okay now... lemme introduce Pramod my BF... my father knows him as well... Pramod meet my sister Sarah and her Boyfriend Kevin"

"Hello" said Pramod with a smile but both Sarah and Kevin wasn't ready to give one in return.

"They are still in shock and disapproval of what I did!" said Serene.

"Sorry from my side for what Serene did. She did it out of parental emotion. Sorry guys. Please make yourself comfortable. I will make sure stay memorable!" ended Pramod making Sarah and Kevin somewhat comfortable.

"Now... I will explain about my routine and Sarah please do say about yours' we are gonna fake each other and need the perfection!"

Sarah nodded not knowing the upcoming play of destiny and started reciting hers' and listening to the others' with unfolded secrets.

VIII

The turn 2

Though Sarah is someone who enjoys the greenery around her, the situation which she is forced to fit into made her clutch Kevin's hand not out of love but out of fear and dilemma whether the decision she took is right or wrong. She wasn't sure whether all these would go properly without any mess. She was in a phobic state of fearing that her nightmare of losing her parents would come true.

All she could think was not to lose them at any cost and also not to share their love with someone unknown. She wished hard for any chance so that she could re think everything and act accordingly. She wished Kevin didn't see her at all and even after seeing so shouldn't have given a damn about Sarah to Serene before knowing her true self. She also couldn't figure out the true nature of Serene and so she wasn't able to sort out the mess happening out there. With all the things taking place in a hurry, she saw Serene singing merrily wandering here and there.

But there in the other end, Serene was in her cloud nine. She was jubilantly running aroound hoping and hugging Pramod out of the sudden burst of excitement. She even saw Sarah battling hard with her emotions and decisions but wasn't ready to enquire and give a change for her to rethink. All she thought is to proceed with the best chance she ever got.

With extremities fighting hard with their ironical feelings, Pramod and Kevin also seemed concerned. Not knowing what to do and where to begin Pramod came to Sarah and broke the morning's ice.

"Hey guys... good morning! How was your stay? Was it comfortable?" asked Pramod occasionally eyeing on Serene and warning her to be careful.

"Yeah good" responded Kevin so glum. Sarah stood still.

Serene seeing them came hurridly waving towrds them.

"Hey babe... meet you in a week... bye..." hugged Serene making Pramod give a nod of acceptance.

"Be careful and don't over expect things. Make sure you are safe and call me if you need anything at any time. I will take care of Sarah and Kevin and you don't worry!"

The way pramod said the last phrase seemed wierd to both Sarah and Kevin and they both looked at each other. Sensing the sudden rush of tensed vibe, Serene filled up the break.

"Thank u so much Pramod. Lucky to have you by my side! please DO take care of my BELOVED sissy and her beloved one!" came a cold fake accent from Serene which was unexpected by the duo.

"Bye sissy and bye Kevin... I'm sorry again for the way I treated you guys and thank you so much for giving me such a memorable and forever cherishable opportunity!" came back her usual softened sugar dipped tone.

Both Kevin and Sarah weren't ready to say anything. They in turn gave a smile and bid her farewell waving their hands. They were confused as hell as they seemed to be choked by all these. Their minds were desperate of taking a pause and restarting things later.

Serene started her journey with all the instructions given by Sarah about her behaviour and things to follow in her home to make sure her parents don't sense anything fishy. Sarah was so clear in that she should never leave a chance to make Serene take over her position. Although Serene was keen in making her forcefully feel the twin vibe, Sarah could feel nothing from her heart.

"Okay then... will take you for a walk afternoon all around the farm... take your time and refresh yourselves. And Sarah make sure you aren't..." started Pramod with a half warning tone.

"So close with the so called manager Kevin..." sighed sarah for Pramod's warning.

Serene had introduced Kevin to everyone as her manager as Sarah insisted Kevin to be with her till she came back from the weeks drama. She felt that she could trust only him and not anyone else around who all seemed to be the wieredest ones she has ever experienced.

"yep... see you later!" saying so went Pramod leaving them behind.

"I'm sorry Sarah" said Kevin with his eyes welling up.

Sarah hadn't seen Kevin feel so low and dejected. She could sense the guilt in his eyes for making her come here and face all these. She wasn't angry at him and could understand him very well. She thought of the excited tone of Kevin when he said about Serene and this painful tone of his'. She really wanted to comfort him eventhough she herself was in the state of reaching out for something to hold up.

"I really didn't mean to do so... I'm..." continued Kevin.

"Kevin! I know... just leave... ***Destiny*** knows what it is doing and what it should... now c'mon lets enjoy this week of unexpected date!" smiled Sarah which made Kevin relieve much.

A week went by and slowly Sarah and Kevin began to regain themselves. They started enjoying the stay with occasional difficulties in managing to be Serene but with Pramod it was much easier. The trio started changing the tense atmosphere into a merry go one. They explored every possible mysteries of nature in that amazing hill and even found themselves lost deep in the jungle of magical heal. Pramod seemed to be a cool and fun loving person. There was no information or hustle regarding Serene replacing Sarah back in home. Time was fleeting and the day of exchange was about to come tomorrow.

"Though I feel pleased about returning back to my normal life, I will definitely miss this." said Sarah as they had the best time together without the fear of being encircled with questions and that too in Sarah's forever love since childhood - the nature and its beauty.

"Yes Sarah, these days and this place is just amazing!" said Kevin wrapping Sarah around his arms.

"I miss mom and dad Kevin" said Sarah laying in the cosy arms of Kevin.

"What?! You say you always feel like going away from them as they used to restrict you much!" tickled Kevin.

"Yes indeed... but their love is truly irreplaceable... the feel of safety and the feel of warmth I had with them is unexplainable..." heartfelt words came from Sarah as she closed her eyes.

"True... But what about this warmth???" asked Kevin playfully

"You are my second best... you idiot!" giggled Sarah.

"SARAHH... SARAHH..."

Startled couple looked above to see Pramod panting towards them with a horror struck face.

"What happened... calm down Pramod"

"SERENE'S DAD IS BACK AND WANTS TO MEET YOU RIGHT NOW!"

IX

The bump

All that Sarah could do was to blame her fate. Her mind started spinning with questions again as if it got struck in a tornado of emotions and tests. "Where the hell does this all take me to?" "Why can't I be happy atleast for a few days all together?" "Am I never ever destined to smile with my heart?" She was so tensed that the only comfort she enjoyed was that she needn't act much around anyone like Serene as she could lock her up in the farms all day saying that she is working. But now...

"What am I supposed to do now?" started Sarah.

"Greet him with a hug as Serene does"

"What should I call him?"

"Papa... that's what she calls"

"Did serene pick up the call?"

"Not yet... I'm trying"

"Pramod I am scared"

Their running walk was halted all of a sudden. Pramod gave the least care about her comment and turned around.

"Kevin... I don't know what is gonna happen there... but you stay here and lemme take Sarah alone... I hope you understand"

Kevin who was following them closely understood the situation and said,

"Take care Sarah... ping me at any time you need... I will come right then no matter what happens!"

'But Kevin... I'm scared..." cried Sarah who had the last hope called Kevin now being deported. She though was afraid had a good feel of her only support Kevin and now... gone!

"You can Sarah... just a day to go... don't worry!"
saying so Kevin went back retracing. He was also deeply in thought and concern about letting Sarah go through this alone. All these days he was determined in making sure Sarah is good and safe in the mess which was his creation at first. But now he is forced to leave her with an unknown to an unknown place to literally act like an unknown.

Meanwhile, Pramod and Sarah reached their home, actually the castle in woods it seemed like. The big red blocks arranged in an old fashioned way which gave it a grand vintage look made her look at it in awe. She felt that the trees are embrassing those bricks with their long arms and rattling among themselves about its texture and amazement. She felt like the trees were competing with it to see who is taller among them.

The big black gate threw open and in there was a whole lot of people awaiting their arrival. The big pool of sea blue water with artificially blown waves seemed like an odd feature into the dark woods. The glass like marbled floor and the true sparkling glasses with intricate and millenial features were catching her attention all at once. While her eyes were busy admiring the ambience over there, her mind gave her a tight slap and brought her back to the hardest reality in front.

"Surprisee..." greeted a man with open arms.

Sarah looked at Pramod who nodded indicating that it is Serene's father.

"Hi papa..." acted Sarah in the best possible way she could.

Mr.Gradon showed his fist as if she was supposed to be a father – daughter bump and Sarah sensing it bumped back.

"Now tell me, where is Serene?" asked Gradon calmly - ***THE SHOCKER WAS JUST SO STRONG THAT IT HIT HER HARD A BIT LATER AFTER BEING PROCESSED.***

"Sorry? Papa... are you... are you joking?" stammered Sarah not knowing what to do.

"WHERE IS SERENE? DID YOU HEAR ME RIGHT?" shouted Gradon with fierce eyes. Sarah was slowly losing consciousness. She felt like something is dragging her deep down into an unending trench.

"I... I... I am Serene papa... right in front of you... Pramod?" she scanned her eyes pleading for a stand from Pramod her only choice.

"Yes uncle... she is..." Pramod who stood there as if he was electrocuted.

"STOP THIS DRAMA AND SAY ME WHERE SERENE IS?!" barked Gradon and grabbed Sarah by neck, chocking her to death.

Pramod who was startled and taken aback by the sudden and unexpected twist, screamed and started saying the truth

"STOP IT UNCLE... SERENE WENT TO SEE HER BIOLOGICAL PARENTS... LEAVING HER TWIN HERE!"

"Pramod!!! noo!!" screamed Sarah. She feared that more than losing her life, her parent's would leave her. Her fear was that Gradon should not call her parents and reveal this mess making them reconsider their decision in anything and everything. She also know that Serene is good in pacifying people and could manipulate even for an exchange with Gradon. All she was strong is that she would never trade anything for her parents.

"Twin?? Serene doesn't have a twin and this girl here in front is ***NOT her twin***!"

"What do you mean? Serene said so and made me stay here!" coughed Sarah with difficulty.

"She doesn't have parents!" blew the whistle for the next shocker ahead.

"They died?" asked Pramod with concern for his love.

"No, there are no parents for her!" repeated Gradon again with a stern look and firey voice.

"What does that mean?" asked Sarah who thought that Gradon also seemed suspecious as like his daughter. sorry! 'so called daughter' of unknown identity now.

"She is an unethical clone created by scientific means. I was the one who created her"

X

The sign of destination

Sarah landed in the ground with a thud. She was of course hoping for the worst but not this kinda worst one. Her mind abandoned her for a while saying that it couldn't handle anymore. Her heart was tired of all the sudden shock waves with such strong magnitudes and that too without any warnings.

Pramod and some of the workers from there grabbed her and rested her on a stone bench out there. Her dizzy eyes were not ready to open wide but she tried hard to do so.

"Sorry papa... I mean uncle... sir... could you please explain this?" murmured Sarah gathering all her remaining bits of energy scattered.

"Back then years ago, I worked as a scientist in a reputed institute. My research gained a lot of best impressions from all people but many weren't ready to recognise my efforts. All they did was mocking me for my work and degrade me with words of discouragement and hopelessness. They strangle me with many hinders which I had to break and spend half of my time on them. Then came the point of saturation in me which made me trust only in my knowledge and confidently quit from the place."

There was utter silence all around as if some crime activity managed to take place over there. Sarah and Pramod were the top class listeners in the school of silence prevailing over there.

“Yes, I was the one who created her. I want to show the world that anything is possible and so I did this. But once I got to know that was unethical and also finding out the aftermath of such creations, I regretted it.”

There were a series of questions piling up in every mind over there but none dared to open up. But Sarah who couldn’t control herself posed the first question which was nagging her all way long =.

“but how come she is like me?”

“I used you for the experiment with your parents consent and that is why”

"What on Earth is happening? Oh God Sarah!" screamed her inner voice.

“But how did she think she has got her parents? Does she know she is a clone?”

“I nurtured her so well as my very own daughter. She grew out to be a normal girl with no abnormalities but her aggressiveness grew along with her well hidden”

“what do you mean?”

“the only difference between you and her is the vein mark in her fist and that is how I found you. She started asking questions about her mom for which I said she is no more. that is the point I found her aggressiveness coming out in rage. When something is said not to be hers’ there comes an uncontrollable rush of emotional anger which makes her lose herself" continued Gradon now with weak voice.

"The fist bump I give is to make sure nothing is abnormal and everything is under control. The vein mark is something which makes me confirm everything. The absence of that in you made me conclude and comprehend everything in a second!"

"so you said her the truth of her being created?" questioned Sarah

"yes...and when she accepted it, she was quite normal but wanted to see her look alike. I couldn't figure out why but destiny showed the answers now"

"so she didn't accept but kept the thought of her parents aside and now when chance showed up she took the advantage"

"exactly... I will never leave her because of this. Her strange behavioural patterns and mood shifts made me examine her from time to time. She started showing various changes and that was the point of concernfor me to reconsider this. I thought of taking her with me wherever I go but out of no choice and to have a secret opinion with my fellow scientists to bring out a solution to this problem but all in vain"

"NEVER GO AGAINST NATURE AS NATURE HAS PLANNED OUR DESTINY Mr.GRADON" came a voice behind

"dad... mom... SERENE!" ran Sarah towards them.

XI

The destin(y)ation

"Steven!" stared Gradon.

Serene was there with a panic striken face and with a very low energy. She couldn't face her father nor the parents which she thought of owning by any means. She stood there alone not even daring to face Pramod who truly loved her and she felt like she betrayed him. Pramod looked at Serene and sense the blended guilt in her face. He turned towards her when Steven gave his reply

"yes it's me Gradon, when Serene came to us, right away we know it wasn't Sarah but without knowing her whereabouts we weren't ready to risk and made Serene stay with us! And once she got emotionally weak she herself confessed the truth and here we are with your daughter, the creation of your science!" slammed Steven.

Sarah was clenching the arms of her father half hiding as if she was a little kid. Her mother was sobbing with happiness and releif. But Steven was fuming with anger not only because Serene but also because of the concent he gave years ago out of the life threat he faced from Gradon.

"SERENE, my dear!" cried Gradon

Serene ran towards him and cried to her might. She felt left out a minute go and not got back a tinge of her ususal confidence. She gathered herself to utter the words of appology to her father.

“Sorry papa... I didn’t mean to...” with tears falling on his hands.

“It’s okay my dear. It’s all my fault which made you both fall into trouble”

There were scenes of true emotions with different personalities placed in positions. After a while...

“Gimme a moment dad” said Sarah approaching a tired and weak Serene hugging Mr.Gradon.

“Serene... it’s not your fault you have been created... it’s not your fault you messed up all these but I can give you something which I can do”

Serene saw her with questioning eyes and tears

“You are a part of me anyway and so you can come and visit us and consider us your family anytime. I will accept you as my sister so will my family.”

With gratitude and love brimming in her eyes as tears Serene looked at Sarah with awe.

“Sorry Sarah!” came a feeble voice yet true apology from Serene.

"It’s okay Serene. There is nothing wrong in longing for a parental care. The most powerful of all. I can truly understand you. Going against the nature can always make every thing go in sixes and sevens. Hope everyone understood it once again. You are not to be blamed. There is nothing for you to feel guilty. As you said you CAN and ARE my twin sissy from now! okay?!!" hugged Sarah.

Steven hugged his smiling daughter saying “Proud of you my dear!!”

Pramod and Gradon there with smiles in their face and contentment. And all set for their routine yet newly fangled versions with hearts of joy!

EPILOGUE

"Sarah... Pramod said everything are you okay... That... Serene... I will... Kill her... you..." came Kevin panting not knowing anything which happened over there.

Startled Sarah was trying hard to sign him but he was too panic striken about Sarah. He came running towards Sarah hugging her with tears.

Mr. and Mrs. Steven were giving her a stern look and then realised Kevin, the strange situation prevailing. Mr.Gordon, Pramod and Serene were trying hard to hold their smile but in vain.

Sarah was neither able to react to Kevin nor to her parents. She hung her head down and stood still. Kevin sensing the mess took a deep breath and went straight to her parents.

"I'm sorry uncle that I have to face you such a situation. I love Sarah and I wish to give her the best life possible. I will never make you feel down for giving me your daughter hand in hand and I assure you that she will smile with her heart forever" completed Kevin.

Sarah was still in shock and was retrieved by Serene.

"Papa... nobody can be a perfect match for Sarah other than Kevin. I have seen it by the way he stood for her till the last and in everything. please do say a positive response. They do need your approval and I am excited to see my sissy's wedding too." supported Serene. For the first time Sarah felt glad that she had a sisterly vibe heartening her.

"Papa... I..." started Sarah

"Stop it Sarah!" came a stern voice from Steven. Her heart sank. She could sense the response.

"but sir..."

"You!! it is all because of you my daughter went through all of this!"

"but papa... without him I wouldn't have survived this hardest journey this long and..."

"I said stop Sarah!"

"I'm sorry sir... but I need your permission too.. I don't want Sarah to be separated from the treasure of parental love. I saw her struggle these days without it and I don't want that to be life long. It is your wish sir... I'm leaving" said Kevin wiping his tears.

"but Kevi... wait!" sobbed Sarah.

"Don't you dare to move away from my daughter!" stormed Steven

Kevin was startled and turned around.

"I may seem like a typical father who wishes to see his daughter getting married to the one he wishes. But I can see that my daughter's choice is right by the way you made up your decision right away. I give you both my consent. Look... I will kill you if you dare make my daughter feel that her decision and choice wasn't right... Got it mister?!"

Sarah ran to hug her father with happy tears. Serene and pramod jumped in joy. Kevin was there transfixed with gratitude brimming eyes.

"So my first visit to our home will be for your wedding... right sissy?!" teased Serene with a bump with Sarah scanning the floor blushing.

That was the happiest roar of laughter with filled hearts.

SCIENCE AND HUMANS MESSED EVERYTHING UP BUT DESTINY SET THEM RIGHT!

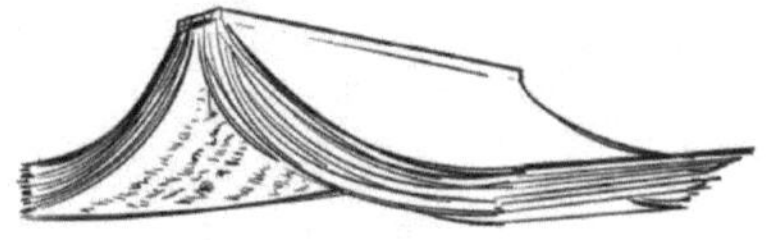

Enter Caption

AUTHOR NOTE

Hello readers,

Hope you all enjoyed reading the work of mine. This little journey of destiny might have inspired you, made you change your perspective towards destiny or might not have any. But it is my pleasure to thank you for chosing this work of mine, the third book of mine. This try of a 24 hr book was my second and first successful try. I feel elated to let you know about 2 of my other books 'RHYTHMS OF A CHARMAINE" and "THE DIARY OF THE PREDILECTED DIDACTICS". Have look at them too. Awaiting your reviews.

Yours

Juno Ashok

Reach me through amjuno2001@gmail.com

9 798889 860693

Printed by Libri Plureos GmbH in Hamburg,
Germany